VIKING
ADVENTURES

OOLAF
THE HERO

Written and Illustrated by Andy Elkerton

W
FRANKLIN WATTS
LONDON•SYDNEY

Franklin Watts
First published in Great Britain in 2017 by
The Watts Publishing Group

Text and Illustrations © Andy Elkerton 2017

The rights of Andy Elkerton to be identified
as the author and illustrator of this Work
have been asserted in accordance with the
Copyright, Designs and Patents Act, 1988.

Series Editor: Melanie Palmer
Series Designers: Peter Scoulding
and Cathryn Gilbert

ISBN 978 1 4451 5818 1 (hbk)
ISBN 978 1 4451 5817 4 (pbk)

Printed in China

Franklin Watts
An imprint of
Hachette Children's Group
Part of The Watts Publishing Group
Carmelite House
50 Victoria Embankment
London EC4Y 0DZ

An Hachette UK Company
www.hachette.co.uk

www.franklinwatts.co.uk

Chapter One

At the far end of the world, right near the edge, was the place where Oolaf Oolafson lived. It was a very special place ...

... because it was full of Viking heroes!

Oolaf's dad was the Village Chief, and the greatest hero of all. He was always going off on adventures and coming back with amazing stories.

... So I pulled its tooth out with my bare hands!

WOW!

Oolaf LOVED hearing stories! Late at night he would sneak out of bed and listen to the Village Storyteller tell tales of terrfiying monsters and daring quests.

"When I grow up I'll go on adventures and people will tell stories about me," Oolaf thought.

Chapter Two

But Oolaf knew that he was still too little to go off on adventures. His mum and dad would never allow it. Being grown up seemed a very, very long way away.

Playing with his favourite toys didn't even make him feel better ... but they did give him a MARVELLOUS idea!

"If I can't go and find an adventure of my very own then I'll bring an adventure to me!" Oolaf thought. He grabbed some parchment and wrote three letters, very carefully in his best handwriting.

Chapter Three

Next morning he took the first letter into the Gloomy Forest.

He pinned it on a pointy branch ... when suddenly there was a terrible growl.

It was the WHITE-WINGED WOLF!

The wolf was getting ready to pounce when Oolaf threw his favourite wooden sword as far as he could.

The sight of a big sword-shaped stick was too much for the wolf to resist and it shot after it! Oolaf ran in the other direction, as fast as his feet would take him.

Oolaf kept on running until he found his little boat, hidden at the water's edge.

He got in and rowed … and rowed … and rowed.

He went much further than he meant to,
where the air was full of flying snikker snaks.

He rowed right up to a swirling whirlpool.

He threw the second letter into the waves,

right down to the bottom of the sea, then

paddled away as fast as he could.

Chapter Four

Oolaf's final letter was for Craggy Mountain.

He began to climb ...

and climb ...

and climb ...

... until he reached the home of the Thieving Ravens. They croaked and pecked, swooping and swiping at him for things to steal.

Oolaf fought them off and left the last letter safely under a rock. Then he slid down as fast as his bottom could take him!

As soon as he got home
he ran up to his room
and waited ...

and waited ...

and waited.

Meanwhile in the Gloomy Forest something pulled a letter off a pointy branch.

At the bottom of the sea something pulled a letter out of a bottle.

At the top of Craggy Mountain something pulled a letter out from under a rock.

17

Dear Dragons
You are the rottenest
Monsters we know.
Your bad breath smells
like a nasty toilet!

Please KEEP AWAY
from our Village.

Signed
The Heroes

Soon the Trolls, Sea Monsters and Dragons were on the move. Oolaf really was about to have the biggest adventure EVER!

The very next morning, a great big
RUMBLE woke Oolaf up.
"It worked. My idea worked!
They're coming!"

RUMBLE
CRASH
THUD

21

Chapter Five

Soon the alarm in the village rang.

"MONSTERS! Lots of MONSTERS!"

The Viking heroes rushed out to see

Trolls, Dragons and Sea Monsters

looking very cross indeed!

Oolaf began to think his three letters were
not such a good idea
after all.

MONSTERS!

Everyone was so busy fighting that they
forgot to look how close to the edge
of the world they all were ... and they
started to tumble over the edge!

Sea Monsters grabbed
hold of Dragons, who clung
on to Trolls, who held on to the
heroes, who held on to Oolaf's dad ...

24

"HELP!" they all
wailed. Oolaf ran
to help. He grabbed
his dad and pulled
and pulled with all
his might, but
no one moved.

THUNK!

"HELP!" they all
wailed again.
Oolaf didn't know
what to do. Then he
heard a strange noise.

THUNK! Sitting there, wagging his tail, was the WHITE-WINGED WOLF and there on the ground was Oolaf's wooden sword.

Suddenly Oolaf had a MARVELLOUS idea!

"Grab hold of his tail, Dad," Oolaf shouted.
Then he climbed onto the wolf's back
and threw his sword up as
high as he could.

Clever Dog!

The WHITE-WINGED WOLF
gave a big flap of his wings and
soared up after it, pulling
everyone to safety.

The monsters were so relieved they were safe that they quite forgot about the letters. They all thanked Oolaf for rescuing them and for having so much fun! Then they all returned to their safe, cosy homes.

When they were alone
again, Oolaf's dad
frowned. He held
up the three
letters.

"Look what I
found," he growled.
"Uh oh!" said Oolaf, shuffling. "Sorry Dad.
I just wanted a big adventure of my own.
I wanted to be a hero, just like you."

Dear Trolls

You are invited to a
Big Hullabaloo
tomorrow,
at The Village
Near the End of the World

We DO hope you can come!

From
The Heros

Dad smiled. He'd
had a FABULOUS
idea! He wrote
three invitations
in his best
handwriting.

29

The next day a bunch of very happy, very noisy, very BIG visitors came to the village holding their invitations to the biggest HULABALOO ever. They had so much fun, they agreed to have one every year ...

... so none of them would forget about little Oolaf – the bravest, cleverest, newest hero from the village at the end of the world.